Yukon Sled Dog

by **Judith Janda Presnall**

illustrated by **Mark Elliott**

two lions

For my grandson Gregory Arthur Milburn
—*J. J. P.*

To Cindy—for being a wonderful wife
and a compassionate friend
—*M.E.*

two lions

Amazon Publishing
Attn: Amazon Children's Publishing
P.O. Box 400818
Las Vegas, NV 89140
www.amazon.com/amazonchildrenspublishing

Library of Congress Cataloging-in-Publication Data available upon request.
ISBN-13: 9781477817315 (hardcover)
ISBN-10: 147781731X (hardcover)
ISBN-13: 9781477867310 (eBook)
ISBN-10: 1477867317 (eBook)

The illustrations were rendered in pencil and colored digitally.
Book design by Virginia Pope
Editor: Marilyn Brigham

Printed in China (R)
First edition
10 9 8 7 6 5 4 3 2 1

On a misty spring night, a newborn husky huddles with her brothers. Puppy Yukon is the only girl in the litter. She grunts with pleasure as owner Roberta cuddles her fuzzy body.

Roberta plans to train Yukon and her brothers to be racing sled dogs.

Sled dogs must love to run.
Sled dogs must be strong.
Sled dogs must obey commands.
Sled dogs must get along
with teammates.

Yukon and her brothers grow fast. Roberta moves them to the puppy pen, where Yukon runs for hours on a puppy-size hamster wheel. Roberta notices Yukon's high energy.

Today is the puppies' first training session.
Roberta takes them for a romp in the woods.
Four big dogs from Roberta's kennel join
the puppies.
   Roberta yells, "Hike!"
The kennel dogs run fast.
Yukon thinks it looks like fun.

Yukon and her brothers run, too.
Roberta hollers, "Whoa!"
The big dogs stop.

Yukon and her brothers smash right into them.

Yukon has grown taller. Roberta takes
the puppies to her kennel. The kennel dogs
welcome them with yips and spins.

Yukon spins, too.

Oops!

Yukon gets tangled in her chain.

The summer heat sizzles. Roberta trains the pups in the cool mornings. She puts a harness on Yukon and attaches a short rope to it. The rope follows Yukon everywhere, snagging on bushes and rocks.

Now Roberta ties a light log to Yukon's rope. The log bounces behind her when she runs, making Yukon stronger.

Roberta feels Yukon's muscles. It is time to test her.

Yukon is on a long leash. "Hike!" Roberta shouts.
Yukon zooms ahead.

"Whoa!" Roberta calls. Yukon stops.

"Good job, Yukon!" Roberta
pats Yukon's head. The pup's
wagging tail whips the air.

Yukon and her brothers practice "Hike!" and "Whoa!" for many weeks. Yukon is faster and smarter than her brothers.

In the autumn the puppies learn teamwork. Roberta snaps Yukon next to her mother. Yukon will learn to lead the team!

Leaders must be smart. Yukon's mother knows "Gee" means "Turn right," and "Haw" means "Turn left."

Yukon learns these new commands.

The team of eight dogs tugs the cart down the trail.

Yukon trains for two long winters. To grow stronger, the team pulls a sled heaped with rocks. Yukon is sturdy, fast, and knows all of her commands.

Is she ready to race?

One dark morning Roberta loads
the dogs into boxes on her truck. She
unsnaps Yukon from her doghouse
chain. The pup prances to the truck.
    Yukon snuggles in her straw-lined box.

When Roberta stops driving, Yukon blinks at the morning sunlight. Waiting dogs yelp and leap with excitement, their breath puffing like smoke in the cold air.

This is Yukon's first race!

Wearing booties to protect their paws, the hitched team lines up. An announcer calls, "Thirty seconds!" Musher Roberta balances on the sled runners, driving Yukon and the dog sled team to the starting chute.

Soon Roberta hollers "Hike!"

The team bolts off, throwing snow from their paws. *Mush! Mush!* Crowds of cheering people disappear behind them.

They race for many hours, stopping only for snacks, until . . .

Uh-oh!

A hare bounds in front of Yukon.

Yukon's mother curls her lips, her low growl warning the team not to leave the trail.

Roberta shouts, "On by! On by!" Yukon and her team stay on the trail.

Roberta sings out praise. "Good dogs! Hike! Hike!"

The team swooshes past another team that has stopped for a snack.

Sunlight is disappearing, and Yukon's team presses on. Mush! Mush!

FINISH

A screaming, clapping crowd welcomes teams at the finish line. Yukon and her team cross second!

Roberta rewards each sled dog with hugs, kisses, and a frozen salmon chunk.

Yukon has proved to be a great leader. She can't wait for her next race.

Author's Note

Sled dog racing wasn't a popular sport until the early 1900s. Before that, Arctic people used sled dogs to transport their household possessions and for hunting seals and caribou. The dogs also aided polar explorers.

In 1925 more than twenty relay teams of sled dogs bravely fought blinding blizzards to take life-saving medicine to children ill with diphtheria in Nome, Alaska. Without those dogs, the children would have died. This event inspired the annual Iditarod Trail Sled Dog Race in Alaska, which began in 1973. The 1,049-mile race starts in Anchorage and ends in Nome.

Today working sled dogs have been replaced by snowmobiles. Sled dogs are now trained for racing and recreation.

Huskies are most commonly chosen for sled dog racing because they have thick coats and strong legs with sturdy, padded paws. They are also skilled at teamwork and following a lead dog.

Training sled dogs involves exercise, cart pulling, conditioning, and sled pulling. By age four months, puppies can travel up to three miles. They run freely with experienced dogs and learn to follow commands. A musher's commands include *Hike* (Go), *Whoa* (Stop), *Gee* (Turn Right), *Haw* (Turn Left), and *On by* (Pass). Some mushers make kissing sounds and whistle, too.

When the puppies are about six months old, the trainer fits each with a harness and attaches a short rope to it. They will wear this harness for roughly thirty minutes every day. Later, a light log is attached to the rope; these exercises get the dogs used to pulling weight.

When the weather cools, the kennel dogs join the puppies for a stronger training program. The puppies, hooked with an experienced partner, learn to run on a towline pulling a wheeled cart. This teaches them teamwork, conditions their bodies, and builds endurance. Finally, when snow covers the ground, they pull sleds, which glide swiftly over the snow. Sleds are loaded with rocks to help the dogs develop balance and agility.

A sled dog's diet of fat (50%), protein (30%), and carbohydrates (20%) is eight hundred calories per day while on summer rest. During a winter long-distance race, a sled dog will eat up to ten thousand calories per day!

It takes a special combination of strength, obedience, and endurance to be a great sled dog. Dogs like Yukon are one of a kind!

Hike, Yukon, hike!